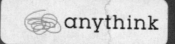

anythink

To all the little Fridas in the world

First U.S. edition 2019
First published by Walker Books Ltd. (U.K.) 2019

Library of Congress Catalog Card Number 2019939112
ISBN 978-1-5362-0933-4

19 20 21 22 23 24 CCP 10 9 8 7 6 5 4 3 2 1

Printed in Shenzhen, Guangdong, China

This book was typeset in Plantin.
The illustrations were done in watercolor and gouache.

Candlewick Press
99 Dover Street
Somerville, Massachusetts 02144

visit us at www.candlewick.com

Little Frida

A Story of Frida Kahlo

ANTHONY BROWNE

CANDLEWICK PRESS

When I was six, I fell ill with polio and had to stay in bed for nine months. It was extremely painful, and when I eventually got better, I could only walk slowly, with a limp. Other children laughed and made fun of me, calling me "Peg-Leg!" whenever I walked past.

I tried to hide my thin right leg with three layers of socks, but it didn't fool anybody.

I was different, and being different made me an outsider.

My father was a photographer, and

sometimes he let me help him in his studio.

I colored many of his black-and-white

photographs. Although it was boring work,

I loved being with him.

Most days, though, in spite of having

three sisters, I played on my own. I was

lonely, but I quite liked being separate.

When I slept, I dreamed of flying. I longed to really fly.

I thought about it all the time. For my seventh birthday,

I asked my parents for a toy plane. For days I could think

of nothing else but flying all around the world.

But when the day finally came, these wings were all I got.

I didn't want to show my disappointment, so I kept

the silly wings on and ran to my room.

As I breathed on the window, it slowly became

misty with condensation. I drew a rectangle on the

glass with my finger. Then I added a handle,

and suddenly it was a door!

I opened the door and stepped through it. I was FREE.

I could run!

I ran and ran and ran until I was completely exhausted.

I was hot and very thirsty. There in

front of me was a dairy. I walked all around

the building looking for a way in, but

I couldn't see one.

Just when I was about to give up and go home,

I noticed a little door. I crawled inside.

And then

I seemed

to be falling

slowly

down into

the depths

of the earth.

At the bottom, a girl was waiting for me. She didn't say anything, not even "Hello," but in a strange way I felt as if I'd known her all my life.

I smiled at her, and she smiled too.

The girl silently started to dance. She was a beautiful dancer, and I talked to her while she gracefully moved around the room. I told her all the secret things I worried about (there were many), and she listened to every word I said.

The girl was a stranger, but she felt so familiar. We sat and laughed together. I laughed very loudly, and she laughed without making a sound. We quickly became the closest friends.

I'd never had a friend before.
It was a wonderful feeling.

After a while, I knew I had to go. We waved goodbye,

and I flew back home, away from the dairy . . .

across the plains, and through the door drawn on

the window. I rubbed out the door and ran to the

farthest corner of the garden.

I sat there and thought about my
journey and my new friend.
I was alone again, but now I was
very happy. I knew that I could
go back and see her whenever
I wanted. She would be there
waiting for me.

From that day I began to paint
the girl, over and over again.
I've visited her many times since
we met, and in a way, I've been
painting her ever since. . . .